Bunyip in the Moon

A TALE FROM AUSTRALIA

Retold by Suzanne I. Barchers
Illustrated by Peter Clarke

RED
CHAIR
· PRESS ·

Please visit our website at **www.redchairpress.com**.
Find a free catalog of all our high-quality products for young readers.

 For a free activity page for this story, go to
www.redchairpress.com and look for Free Activities.

Bunyip in the Moon: A Tale from Australia

Publisher's Cataloging-In-Publication Data
(Prepared by The Donohue Group, Inc.)

Barchers, Suzanne I.
    Bunyip in the moon : a tale from Australia / retold by Suzanne I. Barchers ;
illustrated by Peter Clarke.

    pages : illustrations ; cm. -- (Tales of honor)

    Summary: When a young woman is captured and brought under the spell of the
feared Bunyip, one brave hunter sets out to save her. And while his bravery is finally
rewarded, it is thought the Bunyip still looks down on people today to bring them under
its spell. An aboriginal tale from Australia.
    Interest age level: 006-009.
    Issued also as an ebook.
    ISBN: 978-1-939656-77-3 (library binding)
    ISBN: 978-1-939656-78-0 (paperback)

    1. Hunters--Juvenile fiction. 2. Animals, Mythical--Juvenile fiction. 3. Incantations--
Juvenile fiction. 4. Courage--Juvenile fiction. 5. Folklore--Australia. 6. Hunters--Fiction.
7. Animals, Mythical--Fiction. 8. Courage--Fiction. 9. Folklore--Australia. I. Clarke,
Peter, 1965- II. Title. III. Series: Barchers, Suzanne. Tales of honor.

PZ8.1.B37 Bu 2015
398.2/73/0994   2014944303

This series first published by:
Red Chair Press LLC   PO Box 333   South Egremont, MA 01258-0333

Printed in the United States of America

WZ1114   1 2 3 4 5 18 17 16 15 14

Long ago, in the time before history, the **Bunyip** freely roamed the land where the Murray River would one day flow. One evening, as night fell, the Bunyip trudged along the river bed under a full moon. It hoped to glimpse something that would serve as its nightly meal.

Tiring, the Bunyip climbed up the river bank. It leaned against a gum-tree, blending with its **mottled** trunk. While resting, it realized that it was not alone. In the nearby swamp, a hunter crouched motionless in a clump of rushes in the swamp. He was nearly invisible thanks to a bundle of rushes tied on his back.

Two unsuspecting ducks paddled by, only to be snatched up by the hunter. With the rushes still tied to his back, the man turned toward his nearby camp, carrying the ducks.

As the hunter passed the gum tree, the Bunyip braced himself, ready to **seize** the man. That slight hesitation proved to be the Bunyip's undoing. Instead of capturing the hunter, the Bunyip caught only a few of the rushes strapped to the man's back.

The terrified hunter scrambled down one bank of the river bed and up the other. He shouted an alarm to his people as he ran toward the camp. The Bunyip seemed to fade into the night, letting the man escape unharmed. In truth, the Bunyip **lurked** in the shadows, watching, waiting.

The people of the camp rushed to meet the hunter. The most anxious was the young woman he was soon to marry. She took the ducks that he still carried and spoke soothing words to him. But when the hunter shared what he had seen, the people simply stared at him with disbelief.

And that is when the Bunyip saw its chance.

The Bunyip leaped forward, seized the young woman, and raced away toward the swamp. The people chased after it, but no human can outrun a Bunyip. The young woman's struggles could be heard by everyone in the camp. But no one could rescue her, especially at night when the Bunyip is at its strongest.

But that wouldn't stop the young man. All night he pondered what he could do to outwit the Bunyip.

Once the next day had dawned, the young man gathered up his spears and headed toward the swamp. He searched until he found the tracks of the Bunyip.

He found an old tree near the Bunyip's tracks.
Next he found and tied some frogs to the tree
branches. Then he hid nearby and waited.
And waited.

All day he waited, and he neither saw nor
heard any signs of the Bunyip or of the young
woman. Once night fell, the hunter went home
to the camp.

The next morning, the young man returned to
where he had found the tracks. The frogs were
gone. Seeing that the Bunyip had eaten them, he
caught several more frogs. Once again, he tied
the frogs to the tree. Once again, he hid nearby
and waited. And waited.

That night he again went home to the camp.
As before, the frogs were gone the following
morning. Day after day he patiently caught
several frogs, set the bait, hid, and waited.

The people of the camp worried about the young man. They needed to move on, taking their camp with them. But the hunter **steadfastly** refused to go with them. He said that one day the Bunyip would come to collect the frogs, and he'd have his chance to save the young woman he loved.

So the people left without him.

One day, a misty rain fell as the man took up his usual post. His patience was finally rewarded. He saw the Bunyip, who thought that night had fallen because of the dark mist and **waning moon.** The Bunyip still carried the girl as he approached the bait.

Though fearfully afraid, the young man stepped out of hiding and faced the Bunyip. The hunter held his ground as the Bunyip roared. The young woman held out her hands to the man, weeping, while he **defied** the Bunyip.

Finally, the young man made his move and threw his spear. But the Bunyip was too quick, and the spear missed its mark. Turning, the Bunyip grabbed the first thing he could reach, one of the frogs. He threw it at the young man, striking him in one eye. Blinded, but determined, the young man hurled another spear, striking the Bunyip in its eye.

Reeling with pain, the Bunyip dropped his hold on the young woman and fled. The man dashed forward to hold her in his arms. But she was under the Bunyip's spell, and in spite of her love for the man, she turned and followed the Bunyip.

The Bunyip tore through the swamp and raced past where the tea trees flowered. He fled by the black-eyed Susans and flannel flowers. He reached the country where the eucalyptus and cypress trees stood, passing by the sleeping country and a mountain.

The young woman blindly followed the Bunyip.
The young man, stumbling with pain and
exhaustion, staggered after them. On and on
they went, the young man falling farther and
farther behind. The Bunyip seemed to be making
his way toward a round hill far in the distance.
The young woman, still compelled by the spell
to follow the Bunyip, stayed close behind him.

As the young man struggled to close the gap, the Bunyip came to a tall gum tree atop the hill. Then, glaring with its one good eye at the man, the Bunyip began to climb.

The young woman hesitated at the foot of the tree. Weary and frightened, she feared that she wouldn't be able to climb such a high tree. While the Bunyip's spell pulled at her, exhaustion held her back. As she wavered, the young hunter pressed forward while holding the gaze of the Bunyip.

The Bunyip found that he couldn't look away from the young man. And there the three stood, with the young man also coming under the spell of the Bunyip. None of this unlikely trio could move. The Bunyip, high in the tree, stared down at the young couple for days as the moon waxed and waned again.

Then, on one fateful day, a fearsome storm came.
It blew down the tree, revealing that the Bunyip
was dead.

The young man and woman, freed from the spell of the Bunyip, slowly returned the way they had come. After wandering for some time, they found their people. In time, they married and raised a family.

Their children are known as frog people. They never destroy frogs. Instead, they leave them as food for the Bunyips so that these fearsome creatures may always be **appeased**.

The next time the moon is full, look up. If you are lucky, you can see the Bunyip with its one remaining eye, high in the sky, winking down at you to bring you under its spell.

WORDS TO KNOW

appeased: soothed, satisfied

Bunyip: a mythical creature, thought to be found in the swamps and creeks of Australia

defied: openly resisted or refused to obey

lurked: to be hidden while watching someone

mottled: marked with spots or patches of color

seize: take hold of suddenly

steadfastly: loyally, faithfully

waning moon: the time after a full moon, when the moon's illuminated area is decreasing

WHAT DO YOU THINK?

Question 1:   Do you think that there is such a creature as a Bunyip? Why or why not?

Question 2:   What other creatures from folktales are like the Bunyip?

Question 3:   Can you think of anything in your own culture that is similar to this story from the original people of Australia?

About Aboriginal Australia

For thousands of years prior to the arrival of Europeans, land across Australia was occupied by different Aboriginal clans. Aboriginal history has been handed down through stories, dances, myths and legends. These tales were history. A history of how the world was transformed into mountains, hills, valleys and waterways. The stories tell how the stars were formed and how the sun came to be, and why there seems to be a face on the moon.

About the Author

After fifteen years as a teacher, Suzanne Barchers began a career in writing and publishing. She has written over 100 children's books. She previously held editorial roles at Weekly Reader and LeapFrog and is on the PBS Kids Media Advisory Board. Suzanne also plays the flute professionally – and for fun – from her home in Stanford, CA.

About the Illustrator

Peter Clarke developed a passion for magical creatures and mystical places at an early age. After attending Parsons School of Design in New York, he worked on visual development for *Dungeons and Dragons* and animated films: *Dinosaur, Brother Bear, Atlantis* and the *Ice Age* films. Peter continues his magical work at Blizzard Entertainment in Irvine, CA.